FUNNY-BUNNY
Bedtime Stories

Written by Hayden McAllister

AWARD PUBLICATIONS – LONDON

Windmill Bread

There was once a windmill and a baker's shop in the middle of Rabbitland. Three rabbits, Rodney, Rudolph and Rosie lived in the windmill.

When the wind blew, the windmill sails moved and turned the millstones which ground the corn. With the corn, Rosie Rabbit made the bread and cakes which she sold in the bakers shop.

Rosie Rabbit baked such delicious bread that soon lots of rabbits came to the shop to buy it.

In no time at all Rosie's bread became so famous that Rodney Rabbit bought a bakers van so he could deliver bread and cakes all over Rabbitland.

As for Rudolph Rabbit: Well, he was just a baby rabbit who liked eating his mummy's cooking.

Captain Bill

Once upon a time there was a family of rabbits who lived on a lonely island. When they wanted to buy some food on the mainland they would row ashore in their small boat. But one day the rabbit's boat sprang a leak . . . . .

Luckily Captain Bill Pelican heard about their plight and said he would do their shopping for them.

Captain Bill flew to the mainland where he filled his beak with fresh carrots and lettuces for his rabbit friends.

That night the rabbits had a delicious meal and Captain Bill stayed to supper and told the rabbits exciting stories about the sea.

Cyril the Squirrel

Every winter Cyril the Squirrel would go to sleep in his tree home. When cold winds blew Cyril would be wrapped up cosily in his blanket of leaves and grass.

Cyril had never seen the snow . . . . . because while the ponds were frozen and the children were making snowmen, Cyril would be fast asleep and dreaming of springtime.

It was only when the weather turned warmer, when the leaves came back to the trees and the spring flowers blossomed that Cyril would at last wake up. Then he would stand in his doorway, stretch himself and yawn – and thank heaven for springtime! Would you like to be a squirrel?

Wishing Well Hill

John and Mary were staying at their Uncle Ben's. One day Uncle Ben took them out in to the countryside in his car. He took them to a lovely place full of winding roads and rolling hills.

One of the hills was called Wishing Well Hill, because on the top of the hill was an old wishing well.

Uncle Ben parked his car at the bottom of the hill and let John and Mary climb up to the top to see the wishing well.

When John and Mary reached the wishing well they found lots of beautiful flowers growing around it.

John didn't really know what to wish for, but then he remembered that Mary wanted a pet rabbit for her birthday, so he wished for that.

A little rabbit hiding at the other side of the well heard John's wish and hopped out!

The Inventor

Professor Dogwatch loves inventing things – anything at all. When his friends come round they always ask what it is? Just recently Maurice Mouse did just that. "What does it look like to you Maurice", said the Professor. "It looks like a machine for taking potatoes, washing them and cutting them in to chips." "Well that's exactly what it is", said Professor Dogwatch, relieved that someone had found another use for his wonderful looking new machine. After having some tea Maurice Mouse went home to bed. But the professor immediately started drawing ideas for this next invention!

Moonlight Serenade

Cindy Cat was sitting up in bed and reading a book . . . .

Cindy had spent a lovely day with her friend Colin Cat. First the two friends had gone roller-skating on the Pussyland Roller-Skating Rink. When they grew tired of roller-skating, Colin took Cindy to the cinema to see a film about a *gigantic* mouse who chased every cat he saw! Finally Colin and Cindy had left their roller-skates in Cindy's front room and had gone for a stroll underneath the stars.

Now Cindy was just settling down to sleep when she heard someone playing a guitar and singing in her garden!

"Who can that be I wonder?" whispered Cindy to herself. Cindy got out of bed and went to the window. Looking down she saw that it was Colin Cat and he was playing his guitar by the light of the moon.

"I left my roller-skates in your kitchen," explained Colin, "and I didn't want to wake you by knocking on the door . . . . So instead I sang to you!"

"Tomorrow I'd like to sing a duet with you," purred Cindy.

Burt and the Drill

Burt Bear had found a pneumatic drill in his cellar. Just for fun, Burt thought he'd test the drill in his garden.

   The noise from his drill was really awful! A squirrel in a nearby tree covered it's ears with its paws to shut out the noise.

   The drill bounced and shook and wobbled and as Burt held on to it, it made his teeth rattle.

   Chunks of earth were flying everywhere. A moment later Burt's drill had burst an underground water pipe and water spouted high into the air!

   A little bird, perched on the fence, couldn't understand what Burt Bear was drilling for.

   The truth was, that having switched on the great big drill . . . . . . poor Burt Bear didn't know how to switch it off again!!

The Garden Swing

Every Saturday, Ruth Rabbit would visit her Uncle Jeff . . . . . .

In her Uncles Jeff's garden was a friendly old tree with some very strong branches. One of these branches hung out over the lawn. Uncle Jeff had fixed two ropes over this branch and tied them to the wooden swing.

When Ruth Rabbit came to see Uncle Jeff she had a lovely surprise when he showed her the swing.

Now every Saturday morning Ruth Rabbit enjoys playing on Uncle Jeff's garden swing.

The Twins

Billy and Willie Bear were twins.

They wore the same clothes and smiled the same smile.

If Willie scratched his head, Billy would scratch his head as well!

When Billy whistled a tune, Willie would whistle it too.

At their birthday party, after a lovely tea, they entertained their parents and friends with some jokes, funny dancing and some acrobatics. They kept together perfectly. "You are twice as good as I expected!" said their proud father.

The Happy Clown

Colin the Clown worked at the local circus. Every night he made people laugh. During the day Colin often went for a walk in the woods.

The animals knew when Colin was in the woods because he would whistle a special tune as he strolled along.

Colin loved walking in the woods. He knew the names of all the birds and the trees and flowers.

In his pocket Colin would carry scraps of bread and nuts to feed the animals and birds in the wood . . . . . .

He would give nuts to the squirrels and mice, and crumbs to the birds. Colin the Clown didn't make the animals and birds laugh, but he always made them happy.

Monkey Business

There was thunder and lightning over Monkey Village. Rain poured down, splashing off the leaves. Small puddles grew into large puddles. Large puddles turned into lakes. The sky grew darker, and the rain still poured down.

"This looks bad," shouted the Chief of the Monkeys, choking on his banana. "We must do something."

"We could re-build Monkey Village on stilts," suggested Wise Monkey.

"Bit late for that," said the Monkey Chief. "Anyone got any better ideas?"

"Let's build a boat," piped up Tiny Monkey. "Then we can float around until the waters go down."

"That's a good idea," admitted the Wise Monkey.

"But what kind of boat?" asked the Chief. "What shape should it be?"

"Why not a banana shaped boat?" said Tiny Monkey.

"A splendid idea Tiny Monkey!" beamed Chief Monkey. "One day you might become Chief Monkey."

"He'll need to eat a lot more bananas before he's big enough," muttered the jealous Wise Monkey.

Wally Woodpecker

From early morning until late evening Wally Woodpecker's beak could be heard as it tapped in the tree tops of Happytree Forest.

Wally sometimes pecked holes in the tree trunks which other birds could use as a nest and this gave Ronald Rabbit a bright idea! He asked Wally to carve out numbers on some flat pieces of wood.

Wally soon went to work, pecking out the numbers for Ronald.

"We can hang the numbers on the tree next to our home," said Ronald Rabbit to his friends. "That will make the postman's job so much easier!"

Picnic in the Sun

"This is perfect for a picnic!" cried Sam Spaniel. "I'll ask Mum to pack me a hamper, then I'll go off to the meadow and have a picnic in the sun!

"Why not take your friend Lucy Mouse with you to the meadow?" suggested Mum.

"Good idea Mum!" said Sam. "I'll carry her in the hamper."

When Sam opened up the hamper in the meadow the first thing he did was to have a nice drink of orange juice. Lucy Mouse nibbled at a sandwich and cried: "Oh! Cheese sandwich! My favourite!"

Pen Pals

Tiddles Cat and Kitty Cat were pen pals.

Tiddles lived in Ireland and Kitty lived in Switzerland, and they both enjoyed writing letters to each other.

When Kitty wrote and told Tiddles that she had been out tobogganing in the snow, Tiddles wrote straight back and said: "I'd love to visit you one day Kitty, and then perhaps we could go tobogganing together?"

The next letter Tiddles received was from Kitty and with it was an airline ticket to Switzerland.

Tiddles packed her woollen scarf and hat, and flew off to Switzerland. On the day she arrived Kitty took her out tobogganing.

"This is great fun!" cried Tiddles as the toboggan whizzed along through the snow.

"When you're tired Tiddles, we can go home and have some milk and a nice slice of swiss roll for tea," said Kitty.

Sam's Snorkel

While he was at the seaside, Sam borrowed his Dad's diving goggles and snorkel.

"I want to swim in the rock pool," said Sam to his Dad. "Will you come and watch me?"

"Okay," agreed his Dad. "You can pretend you're a submarine."

When Sam swam for the first time under water, everything looked so different! He could hardly believe his eyes when a fish swam towards him.

"Dad's snorkel helps me to breathe under water," thought Sam, "but I wonder how all the sea animals manage to breathe under water *without* a snorkel?"

Baby Bear

Baby Bear was lost in the Big Wood. He'd been walking for nearly an hour and he didn't know where he was.

Mother Bear had said: "Don't go far. And be sure you're back for tea."

"Oh I do wish I'd listened to Mother Bear," moaned Baby Bear. "I would be home now and eating some of her famous honey cake instead of being lost in the Big Wood."

He was just about to lie down and go to sleep when a bumble bee came buzzing by.

"Excuse me Mr Bumble Bee," said Baby Bear, "but can you guide me home please?"

"Of course Baby Bear," buzzed the Bumble Bee. "It's easy. Just follow me. I can smell Mother Bear's delicious honey cake from here!"

Heatwave

It was such a *hot* day. Bob the Bear didn't even have the energy to make himself a honey sandwich. Instead he sat in his armchair with his feet in a bowl of cold water. Around his head he wrapped a towel which had also been dipped in cold water.

In his hand he held an orange drink with some ice cubes in it.

"I'm *so* hot in this heatwave!" moaned Bob. "Next year I'll have to take a *holiday* in Polar Bear Land."

Rainbow Treasure

Maurice Mole could see the end of a rainbow right ahead.

"Everybody knows there's a pot of gold at the end of a rainbow," gasped Maurice. "If I hurry along I might find it."

Maurice scampered along, running as fast as his legs could carry him. Suddenly he found himself standing right under the end of the rainbow.

The colours were marvellous! Maurice had never seen anything so beautiful in all his life.

He was so delighted that he forgot all about looking for the pot of gold!

Bob's One Man Band

Joe and Isabel were walking with their Mum when they heard a sound like a brass band. Looking down the road Joe and Isabel were amazed to see that only one man was making the sound.

"It's Bob Busker and his one-man band," said Mum. "Go and give him this coin and ask him to play a tune for you."

Joe and Isabel ran down to where Bob was standing with his dog.

"And a jolly good day to you!" said Bob, rattling his tambourine.

"Please play us a tune Mr Busker," said Isabel.

"Which tune would you like?" said Bob.

"Would you play 'How much is that doggy in the window'?" asked Joe.

"Well, that's my jolly little dog's favourite tune!" beamed Bob Busker. "Just you watch him wag his tail when I play it!"

Underwater Rabbit

Professor Bobtail was a very clever rabbit. (He knew that the moon is not made of cheese and that carrots don't grow on trees).

Professor Bobtail knew many things, but he didn't know what lived underneath the waves of the sea. So he built his own submarine so that he could sail under water.

The professor's submarine had a big window in it because he wanted to see exactly who lived under the waves.

One day Professor Bobtail took his submarine out to sea and dived under the waves. He looked out of his window and found, to his surprise, an octopus and a dolphin, and lots of fish who were all staring at *him*.

After all, it wasn't every day they saw a rabbit under the sea!

Acorn Soup

Sandra Squirrel had borrowed a recipe book from the Woodland Library. The first recipe in the book told her how to make acorn soup. "I'll need one cup of water, six ears of wheat and some dried acorns," said Sandra. "I think I'll go to the wishing well to draw some water." When Sandra arrived at the well she met Bertie Bird. "Oh! Hello Sandra!" chirped Bertie. "I've just made a wish that someone will invite me to dinner."
"You're very welcome to come and try some of my acorn soup for your dinner," smiled Sandra.

The Wet Mouse

Monty Mouse had been exploring the garden. He was searching for a cool shady spot where he could escape from the heat of the sun.

The clump of big flowers in Lucy's garden was just what he was looking for! Monty curled up beneath the scented flowers and soon fell asleep.

Monty had only been asleep for five minutes when he felt drops of water falling on his furry head. When he stood up he realised that Lucy was watering the flowers.

"Hum! Now I'll have to go and sit in the hot sun to dry off!" muttered Monty.